The Adventures of

Sally the Kiwi

by Ashlee Craft

Freedom Meadow Media

Published by Freedom Meadow Media

Cover art by Ashlee Craft

ISBN-13: 978-1490424811

ISBN-10: 1490424814

It was a hot and sunny day, the type of day where the trees and flowers droop and it's so warm that even the birds are silent.

Sally, who was a kiwi bird, was standing in her yard with her little brother James and her best friend Denny, both of which were also kiwi birds. Although their parents had told them it was a nice day to go play outside, none of the kiwis thought so. It was summer break, and although summer should have been a time when everything was fun and anything was possible, this summer was different.

It was a month into their summer break and none of the friends had ever been more bored in their lives. In fact, sometimes Sally thought they would be having more fun if they were at school. At least when they were at school there was always something to do. Sure, summer break had started out being fun. The friends had raced around in the sprinklers, gone swimming, ate ice cream, played baseball, read books, and played in Sally's yard until dark. Eventually, they had already done everything fun you can do in the summer and were now bored.

It was on this especially hot day that Sally, James, and Denny were sitting in Sally's yard, trying to decide what to do.

"We could go eat ice cream again." Denny suggested half-heartedly.

Sally and James shook their heads.

"I'm tired of eating ice cream." James said.

Sally thought about every type of summer activity and tried to find something that they hadn't already done yet. Still, no matter how hard she thought about this, she couldn't think of anything.

Sally sighed. It seemed like their summer would be wasted sitting in the hot sun and doing nothing.

James said,

"It's too hot in the sun. I'm going to sit under that bush over there."

"Okay." Sally replied.

James walked away, heading for the shady bush that grew in the corner of the yard.

Denny looked at Sally and said,

"What do you think we should do today? I'm bored of being bored, but at the same time, I'm too bored to do anything."

"I'm too bored to think." Sally agreed.

Suddenly, James came running back over towards Sally and Denny and began jumping up and down with excitement.

"Guess what! Guess what!" He exclaimed.

Sally said,

"What is it?" She assumed that James had probably just found a worm or something.

James shouted,

"I found a treasure map! A treasure map!"

Excitement filled Sally and Denny. A treasure map?

"Where?" Denny asked.

"Under the bush!"

Sally, Denny, and James hurried over to the bush in the corner of the yard. Sure enough, under the thick green branches, sat a piece of old looking paper. James said,

"I was digging by the base of the bush, hoping to find bugs, and suddenly I came across a piece of paper! I opened it up and it has a map on it!"

Sally picked up the piece of paper and opened it. The paper was yellow and crinkled, and on its surface was a series of lines, blobs that represented trees and rivers, and a large red "X".

Sally and Denny started jumping around too. They couldn't believe that they had actually found a real treasure map!

When they finally calmed down, Denny asked,

"What should we do now?"

Sally thought for a moment, then replied,

"We should follow it and see where it leads!"

The kiwis hurried inside their house. Sally and James' parents were at work (Sally was happy that she was now old enough to watch over her little brother, as this meant they had a lot more freedom in the summer). They quickly packed some sandwiches and loaded them into Sally's green plastic backpack. They packed a flashlight, picnic blanket, some water, and some plates to bring along as well. They left a note to let Sally's parents know where they had gone. Next, they headed out the door, through the gate in the backyard, and into the forest.

The friends looked at their map and decided which direction they should go. With that, they began walking.

The forest was much cooler than the backyard had been. The tall trees shaded them from the sunlight and the forest was moist and soon, they felt much cooler. Birds chirped overhead, filling the air with pretty sounding music, and the leaves on the ground crunched as they walked over them.

Sally, being the oldest one there, led the way and carried the map. James and Denny hopped along happily behind her.

"I wonder where the map will lead us!" James exclaimed.

"What kind of treasure do you think we'll find?" Denny asked. "I hope there are some old coins."

Sally smiled. Denny had a large coin collection that he kept in his bedroom and he was always looking for new additions to it.

Sally said,

"I bet there will be tons of coins in all shapes and sizes. I hope there's gold too! Maybe the map will lead us to some hidden pirate treasure!"

James squeaked happily at this thought.

The friends were very excited, as they had never been on any real adventures before, and they were so happy that this was finally happening. Sally, James, and Denny had pretended to go on many adventures before, imagining everything from pirate ships to ancient lands.

Sally couldn't believe that only twenty minutes earlier, they'd been sitting in her backyard, thinking that this summer would be their most boring yet. So much had changed in such a short period of time!

The friends hiked on, checking their map every once in a while to be sure they were going in the right direction. When they reached one of the places shown on their map, such as a river or an old tree, they knew they were getting even closer to their treasure and became even more excited.

Eventually, the kiwis became hungry and decided to stop for lunch. Sally and Denny spread the red picnic blanket on the ground while James unpacked their sandwiches, which were made out of insects, as that's one of the things kiwis like to eat. James put the green plates on the tablecloth and put the food on the plates. Next, the kiwis began eating.

"Let's pretend we're pirate adventurers!" Denny suggested as he began eating.

"Great idea!" Sally agreed. "It will make it even better when we do find the treasure!"

Sally really hoped that they would find the treasure. She was aware that they could reach the "X" only to find that there wasn't any treasure there, but she hoped this wasn't true.

She shivered with happiness as she thought about how fun it would be when she got back to school and could tell her classmates all about her adventures. They would be so jealous! Her classmates always had summers much more exciting than Sally's, but for once, her story would be the best.

The kiwis ate their food, talking about what they would do when they had the treasure.

"I want to buy a mansion!" James said. "And a speedboat!"

Denny replied,

"That sounds cool, but I think I'm going to buy a houseboat and travel all over the world on it!"

Sally smiled.

"I want to use my money to build the biggest best treehouse ever and help other kiwis have awesome summers too."

"Great ideas!" James said.

The kiwis finished their lunch and packed the plates and tablecloth back into Sally's backpack. Then, they continued on with their journey, wondering how soon it would be before they came across the treasure.

After a while of walking, the friends stopped to consult their map. They were more than halfway to the treasure by now, and with every step they took, their spirits rose even further. Sally figured that in an hour or so they would reach the "X", and this knowledge inspired her and her friends to walk even faster.

After a while of walking, James became bored.

"How about we sing a song?" Sally suggested.

"Okay." James said. "What song?"

"A pirate song." Sally said, then began singing:

We are pirates on an adventure

On a hot sunny day we look high and low

In less than an hour we'll reach the X

There will be a great treasure there we know

Yo ho ho! Yo ho ho! Yo ho ho

We're pirates!

Sally started singing this verse again, and Denny and James joined in. When they finished this verse, Sally came up with another one:

We were so bored, we had nothing to do

But then James found a map in our yard

We began walking and followed the treasure map

We'll make it there even if it's easy or hard

Yo ho ho! Yo ho ho! Yo ho ho

We're pirates!

The friends continued singing these verses. James shouted the loudest on the "yo ho ho" parts, and Denny helped him with the lyrics if he forgot.

Time passed quickly as the kiwis sang. In what seemed like only a few minutes but was really close to an hour, Sally suddenly realized that they were getting very close to the "X".

"We're almost there!" She shouted. "Everyone, look around and see if you can find an "X"! It might be painted or it might be made out of sticks or rocks, but it must be here somewhere!"

The friends spread out across the area, scanning the ground for any sign of the X or the treasure. When they had carefully searched this area, they walked on a little further and searched the next area.

"Do you think we're in the right place?" Denny asked. "You don't think we've gone too far, do you?"

Sally was just about to answer when the ground suddenly disappeared from underneath Denny and Denny fell into a hole!

Sally and James rushed towards the hole. Sally noticed the hole had been carefully disguised by branches, leaves, and sticks so that it looked like part of the ground.

She peered down into the hole.

"Denny! Denny! Are you okay?" She yelled.

A second later, she heard Denny coughing. It was dark inside the hole and she couldn't see him.

"I'm okay!" Denny called back.

"Are you hurt?" Sally asked.

"No, I'm fine."

"What's it like down there?" James asked.

"I seem to be inside some sort of tunnel!"

Excitement filled Sally. Where did the tunnel lead? Was there treasure down there?

"Denny, get out of the way. We're coming down there!" She shouted.

Denny moved out of the way. Sally got close to the edge of the hole, took a deep breath, closed her eyes, and jumped.

She fell for several seconds before landing in the bottom of the hole. A cloud of dust rose up when she landed, and she coughed too. After brushing the dust off her feathers, she told James to jump.

James landed in the hole next to his friends. At this point, Sally remembered that she had brought a flashlight, and turned it on.

The light from the flashlight illuminated the entire tunnel they were in. It was a tunnel carved out of the dirt and wasn't much taller than the kiwi's heads.

A shiver of excitement passed over Sally. James and Denny stared at her, wondering what to do next.

Sally saw that the tunnel continued on to her right, and she said,

"Let's go see where it leads!"

Sally led the way. She was a little afraid of what might be inside the tunnel, but her excitement was stronger than her fear.

The friends walked down a winding maze of tunnel. The tunnel seemed to go on forever, and Sally wondered if they would ever reach the end of it.

Suddenly, the ceiling got a little taller. Sally shined her flashlight beam up and saw they had arrived in a large underground room.

On the far side of the room was a large pile of gold!

"We found it!" Sally yelled, her words echoing in the tunnel.

She hurried into the room, her friends following behind her just as quickly.

The pile of gold was much taller than the kiwis were. The gold sparkled beautifully when Sally shone her flashlight at it, and the sight was so amazing that the kiwis were awestruck and speechless. They had never seen anything so amazing in their entire lives. It was so wonderful that for a minute, none of them could believe that it was really real.

"Wow." Sally finally said, still feeling speechless.

The kiwis approached the pile of gold. Denny picked up a coin in his beak and shouted,

"This will be perfect for my collection!"

James suddenly said,

"Look! A ladder!"

Sure enough, there was a large wooden ladder leaning up against the pile of gold. This ladder would allow them to get out of the tunnel when they reached the entrance again!

"What do we do now?" James asked.

Denny saw some orange canvas sacks in the corner by the door and realized that these would be perfect for bringing their treasure home in. He gave one sack to each of his friends and took one for himself. The kiwis loaded as much gold as they could into the sacks. When the sacks were full, they set them down and picked up the ladder. They carried the ladder through the tunnel and propped it up against the wall near the opening.

After that, the Kiwis hurried back through the tunnel, returned to the treasure room, put the sacks of gold on their backs, and carried them towards the opening. When they reached the opening, they climbed up the ladder and back into the sunlight. Sally helped her friends out of the hole, and when they were all standing in the forest again, they all regarded the hole with a look of wonder.

Sally, James, and Denny then turned around, looked at their map, and began heading back towards their home, carrying their gold and grinning from ear to ear.

The journey back home didn't seem as long as the journey there. Now that they had found treasure, everything seemed even more amazing than it had before. From time to time, they would check their map to be sure they were heading in the right direction.

Finally, they reached Sally and James' backyard again. It seemed so long ago that they had been sitting there, thinking that there day would end up being boring. It all seemed so amazing that they had really gone on an adventure and found treasure that, had it not been for the sacks of gold on their backs, none of the kiwis would have believed it was true.

They took the gold inside and put the sacks down on the floor. In less than an hour, Sally and James' parents would be home. The kiwis looked forward to telling their parents all about their adventures. Maybe Denny could stay over for dinner!

James suddenly said,

"I'm thirsty."

Sally and Denny decided to make a pitcher of lemonade. When this was made, they poured it into glasses and sat out on the back porch to drink their lemonade.

"Today was the best day ever!" James shouted.

Sally and Denny agreed. It had been the best day ever.

"Everything turned out perfectly. That's the most fun I've ever had! I never thought something like that would happen to me!" Denny said, taking a sip of his lemonade.

Sally nodded in agreement, then said,

"If summer is this amazing already, just think — there's still more time for more adventures, more treasure, and more fun!"

Her friends nodded.

"Let's plan what we'll do tomorrow." Denny suggested.

As the kiwis drank their lemonade and began planning what they would do for the rest of the best summer ever, Sally realized something.

The day had started out boring, but this changed due to a little luck, a spirit of adventure, and most importantly, great friends to share it with.

About the Author

Ashlee Craft is an author, musician, artist, actress, photographer, and poet. She was born in the Pacific Northwest and has always enjoyed writing and music. She loves kiwi birds and hopes to find buried treasure someday too.

29890465R00017

Made in the USA
Lexington, KY
04 February 2019